Tove Jansson

The Dangerous Journey

a tale of Moomin Valley

TRANSLATION BY SOPHIE HANNAH

ENFANT

For Malin and Mikael

drawnandquarterly.com

First Drawn & Quarterly edition: April 2018
Printed in China
10 9 8 7 6 5 4 3 2 1

Library and Archives Canada Cataloguing in Publication. Jansson, Tove. [Farliga resan. English]. *The Dangerous Journey* / Tove Jansson. Translation of: Den farliga resan. ISBN 978-1-77046-320-2 (hardcover). 1. Comics (Graphic works). I. Title. II. Title: Farliga resan. English. PZ7.7.J35Dan 2018   j741.5'94897   C2017-905444-9. Published in the USA by Drawn & Quarterly, a client publisher of Farrar, Straus and Giroux. Orders: 888.330.8477. Published in Canada by Drawn & Quarterly, a client publisher of Raincoast Books. Orders: 800.663.5714

Susanna woke one morning
Bored and confused and cross.
She gave her cat a warning.
She told it who was boss.

You're old, Cat, and you're lazy –
Too peaceful, too serene.
Not me! I'm wild and crazy
And I'm sick of all this green:

She called it to a meeting
Out in the field of flowers.
'Cat, you are always eating!
You munch, then snore for hours!

A field, a tree, a petal –
Quite beautiful, it's true,
But I'm far too young to settle
For nothing much to do.

I'd love it if some vandal
Turned green to sparkling gold –
Danger, disaster, scandal!
What might our future hold?'

Cat yawned and didn't answer her. Susanna felt quite sick.
He made so little effort, it was getting on her wick.
Susanna took her glasses off in order to escape
From the sight of her annoying pet's contented napping shape.
What was this? Another pair
Of glasses had appeared,
Yet nobody had put them there.
'Weird,' thought Susanna. 'Weird.'

She put the glasses on, since hers were nowhere to be found,
And got a shock – instead of lying idly on the ground,
Cat was a spitting frizz of rage, rotating in the sky
With furious jaws and scratchy claws and fireballs in his eye.
'Sorry, Kit,' Susanna cried.
'Don't go. I didn't mean it.'
She wondered if her eyes had lied,
But no – she knew she'd seen it.

She ran towards the forest that she played in all the time.
Help! It was gone. The trees weren't there. Now there was just wet slime.
The forest was a mangrove swamp, all dark and dank and strange.
Susanna wished she'd never asked for anything to change.
Water mirrored back her face
In an alarming manner.
'Who's this wildcat in my place?
And where is nice Susanna?'

What were those tracks across the ground? Oh, no! Oh, please, not snakes!
Snakes are the worst - they're worse than mud and monsters and mistakes.
'Please get me out of here!' Susanna bellowed at the sky.
'I've got the point. I've had my fill. Soon I will start to cry.'
'Calm down - we're the harmless kind,'
One little grass snake said.
Susanna left them all behind
And trembled as she fled.

The sky was full of hot red clouds. Birds flew without a sound.
The beach was still. Susanna heard the silence all around.
She spotted footprints in the sand. 'Oh, help,' she cried. 'A beast!
Or - yikes! - a cat, my sharp-toothed cat, seeking a human feast!'
'Time to head for home,' she thought.
'Proceed without delay.
Adventure? Yes, but not this sort.'
Yet something made her stay.

Beside the cliff, beneath the rocks, the sea had drained away.
No wet, no blue, no waves, no splash - it was as plain as day
The sea was gone, and, in its place, only a gaping void-
A dreadful sight (but one Susanna secretly enjoyed).
'I've got special powers,' she smiled.
'All this is down to me.
I'm just a little girl, a child,
But my mind has moved the sea.'

She wandered on, determined to explore the bright unknown
And met a hefty HEMULEN. He wasn't on his own,
But with a gang - one rather shy, two almost twins, both short.
'If I decide they're nice, then they'll be nice,' Susanna thought.
'Hope's the only way to win.
I've figured out the deal:
First you put your order in
Then your dream turns real.'

HEMULEN said, 'Susanna, hi!' Susanna said, 'I guess
You're rushing to a party, and it must be fancy dress.'
'No, no,' said HEMULEN. 'In fact, we always look like this.
We're on our way to see a friend whose house is hard to miss.
We've missed it, though, which rather grates -
Missed berry-picking too.'
'Poff scancakes,' squealed his near-twin mates.
What did they mean? Who knew?

HEMULEN, Bob and *Thingummy* - those were his friends' strange names -
All clustered round Susanna for some gossip, fun and games.
HEMULEN's timid dog joined in, in his own whispery way.
'This place looks wrong,' said HEMULEN. 'I'd swear that yesterday
Birds weren't flying back to front,
Blueberries weren't lime green.
Life's turned loopy! To be blunt,
It's not at all my scene.'

Bob quite agreed. 'A mightful fress! Hite quorribly foncusing!
Whoever's glaying pames with us, they're linning and we're wusing.'
Susanna said, 'I'm awfully afraid that I'm to blame.
I only sat down in the grass, while things were still the same...'
Then there was a frightful roar
As if the world was making
More noise than it had made before.
The ground would not stop shaking.

SNIFF galloped into view, on fire. 'My tail's too hot!' he yelped.
A hundred HATTIFATTENERS hid who really should have helped.
'Preposterous twits,' cried HEMULEN. 'Those hatfats – what do they know?
Cancel all this – it's pure skew-whiff. That's not the right volcano!'
Thingummy muttered, 'Flazing blame.'
Bob said, 'It's hed hed rot!
Smorld up in woke – a sheadful drame,
When smorld is all we've got!'

Once they had stopped **SNIFF** panicking – he really was uptight –
They headed west to visit friends. Did west mean left? No, right.
No, wrong – their Moomin chums lived either in between that gap
Or... oh, who cares? You'd have to be a fool to trust the map.
Silence from the poor conked-out
Volcano. When not oozing
Lava like a frenzied spout,
He's pretty keen on snoozing.

Night fell and snow fell, pounding like the drumsticks of a drummer.
HEMULEN cried, 'Delete! Rewind! It's still the height of summer!'
The looming shadow of the GROKE, face frightful in the fog,
Did nothing for the confidence of HEMULEN's small dog.
Hiding in Susanna's hug
Was all that he could do.
The dog's last name was Moanymug
His first was Sorry-oo.

'I'm cold,' whined SNIFF. 'I've half a mind to light my tail again.'
Then Thingummy and Bob said words, but only one in ten
Made sense to anyone at all: 'We're frabsolutely eezing!
Let's go hack bome for nice drarm winks, and please don't think we're teasing!'
Did they take their own advice?
The path became a slipping
Mirror made of silver ice
And every nose was dripping.

Two jolly chaps sat snug and warm around a boiling pot
Of brussel sprout and onion soup, lovely and thick and hot.
'Selicious Doup,' said Bob. 'Perfection for a tumbling rummy!'
HEMULEN understood. He said, 'Bob thinks your soup smells yummy.'
'Tail's on fire again!' SNIFF wept.
'It's like the bad old days.
I blame my friends — they're all inept!'
Susanna tamed the blaze.

They ate a ton of soup, then settled down to have a doze—
A normal and appropriate reaction, I suppose.
Snufkin and Wimsy dealt out cards inside their glowing den.
Outside, wolves sang in harmony with howling winds, and then
Late that night, at 2 o'clock,
Sniff woke up feeling sick.
'Onions!' he cried. 'My tum's in shock!
Oh, what a nasty trick!'

Next morning they set off without directions or a map.
(SNIFF hid beneath his quilt, which very nearly caused a scrap.)
SNUFKIN's advice that eastwards was the only way to go
Turned out to be the wrong advice. **Sorry-oo** cried, 'Oh, no!
What a strange and jagged land!'
He got in quite a state.
No one else could understand
His need to relocate,

Until they heard hard snorts and grunts from further up the street
And thuds that brought to mind an angry monster's thumping feet.
They ran away (as people scared of monsters tend to do).
SNIFF whimpered, 'Stop! I think I'm coming down with stomach flu!'
Can our story wait for him?
I'd interrupt this rhyme,
But there's a waterfall to swim,
And we're running out of time.

The snorting creature's chasing them. Why? They've done nothing wrong!
If they're as small and scared as this, he must be huge and strong.
They hear his breath. They smell it too. Help! He will catch them soon!
But what's this dropping from the sky? A red and gold balloon!
'Climb aboard a flying dream,'
A cheery voice calls out.
'It's not as hard as it might seem
If you know what you're about.'

It took a while for **Sorry-oo** to wind and pack his tail.
Tooticky, who was piloting the red balloon, set sail
For shore. With flair and energy, she steered with all her might.
As they escaped, they saw the snorting beast – a gruesome sight!
'Look!' Susanna cried. 'The sea!
Balloon, swing – that's an order!'
But HEMULEN weighed twelve stone three,
So the red balloon ignored her.

'We've got to lose some weight,' Tooticky told the gang. 'The rocks
You've all got in your pockets or your hankies or your socks
Will have to go.' 'Please, no!' SNIFF wailed. 'My diamonds aren't to blame!
It's great big dobbing HEMULEN – his kind are all the same!'
One by one, the jewels were tossed.
Poor SNIFF went quite doolally.
His friends said, 'Everything you've lost
You'll find in *Moomin Valley*.'

Without **SNIFF**'s jewels, the red balloon felt positively slender.
Everyone sensed that scrumptious treats were on today's agenda.
They flew past mountains. There was *Moomin Valley*, bathed in sun.
Sorry-oo whooped with joy, and he was not the only one.
Bob sighed, 'Lovely drilky mink!'
HEMULEN sighed, 'Warm toffee!'
Thingummy said, 'Hey, Suse, I think
You'll love their cot hong stroffee!'

Everyone cried, 'Balloon! Balloon! Quick, catch it! Grab the rope!'
And Moominpappa, on the roof, peered through his telescope
While Moominmamma waved from the veranda's bright blue door.
The grass, if you can credit it, was greener than before.
They landed in a tulip field.
'Steady,' warned Moominpappa
'There's my cat!' Susanna squealed.
'My furry full-time napper!'

'Good afternoon.' Susanna curtsied, keen to get it right.
Now was the time, she thought, to be impressively polite.
'Look at her!' giggled LITTLE MY. 'How strange! Why does she look
Exactly like a character you'd find inside a book?'
BOB groaned, 'Suse, I nid you kot,
MY's the weirdest girl alive.
Mymble! WHOMPS! Whole lolly jot!
Hey, MOOMINTROLL! High Five!'

They had a lovely party – well, what else should they have done?
(They throw a party every day, quite often more than one,
Sometimes outside beneath the stars, or, when it's cold, indoors.)
Then, 'Hometime!' said Susanna. 'Are you coming, Mr Paws?'
Whether things turned out okay
She's never going to know.
When adventure comes your way
Enjoy it. Let it go.